# INTRODUCTION

Yellowstone Park has the largest population of elk in the world.

Elk are among the largest animals in the deer family.

Every fall at Yellowstone Park, the elk bugle to tell of the coming of winter.

# I AM AN ARO PUBLISHING
## 40 WORD BOOK

## MY 40 WORDS ARE:

| | |
|---|---|
| A | is |
| and | know |
| all | let  lets |
| Bugle  bugles | little |
| blows | like |
| blew | must |
| but | not |
| be | snow |
| critters | said |
| can | someone |
| cold | time |
| do | the |
| elk | them |
| for | to |
| flute | told |
| how | toot  tooted |
| he | us |
| have | winter |
| I | when |
| it | Yellowstone |

ISBN 0-89868-177-4 — Library Bound
ISBN 0-89868-178-2 — Soft Bound

YELLOWSTONE CRITTERS

# BUGLE ELK & LITTLE TOOT

## BY BOB REESE

ARO PUBLISHING

**How do Yellowstone critters know,**

It is time for winter and the snow?

**Bugle Elk lets them know.**

Bugle, bugles when he blows.

"Is it time for winter?"
said Buffalo.

"Is it time for Bugle
to let us know?"

"A'choo," said Bugle, "a'choo a'choo."

"A'choo," said Bugle when he blew.

"I can not bugle. I have a cold.

**But all the critters must be toid!"**

"I can bugle," said Little Toot.

"I can bugle like a flute."

"Toot toot toot toot.  Toot toot toot toot.

Toot toot toot toot.   Toot toot toot toot."

"Is it time for winter?" said Buffalo.

"Is it time for Bugle to let us know?"

"It is time for winter and the snow.

Someone tooted
to let us know."

23